For the Love of
Lettuce

Courtney Dicmas

On the same leaf, on the same day, two VERY different caterpillars hatched, side by side.

One was called Zip

and the other,
Parsley.

Zip liked routines.

Every day, he liked to do the same things

and eat lettuce for breakfast, lunch and dinner.

Parsley was the opposite.

Zip liked to plan,

while Parsley just dived right in.

"...LETTUCE!"
huffed Zip.

"Oh dear," burped Parsley.
"Have we run out?"

"Luckily," smiled Zip, "I have a plan."

"WOW!" cried Parsley.
"Look at all that lettuce!
What are those little fluffy things?"

BAWK

"They're chickens," replied Zip. "They're bigger close up.
They have huge eyes and sharp beaks. And they eat caterpillars!"

"I'm not scared of them,"
said Parsley. "Let's go
and find that lettuce!"

The journey to the lettuce garden took a while.

HELLOOOO

Parsley enjoyed every minute of it.

"This is taking too long," moaned Zip. "You've stopped every two minutes to rest, or eat, or play!"

"It's been a lovely day," replied Parsley.

"OF COURSE you would think that!" Zip said crossly.

"All you do is have fun, while I do all the planning. Things need to CHANGE around here!" Zip hollered.

"Do they?" smiled Parsley. "I think things are fine as they are."

Zip tried tickling...

and shouting...

but there was no response.

"Maybe I was too cross," thought Zip.
"I miss you, Parsley. And I don't have a plan for this!"

"Maybe we'll just sit here for a bit."

"What would YOU do, Parsley?" wondered Zip.
"I'll try to think like you for once."

For the first time, Zip noticed the soft rush of wind...

touched the cool softness of flowers...

HELLOOOO

...and heard the soft cluck of chickens.

"CHICKENS?"

"Now what?" thought Zip.

"There's got to
be a good way
out of this!"

BOING

"But this isn't it!"

Zip tried to calm down...

and think like Parsley.

"Where IS Parsley, anyway?"

"Don't worry, Zip," called Parsley.
"I've got you!"

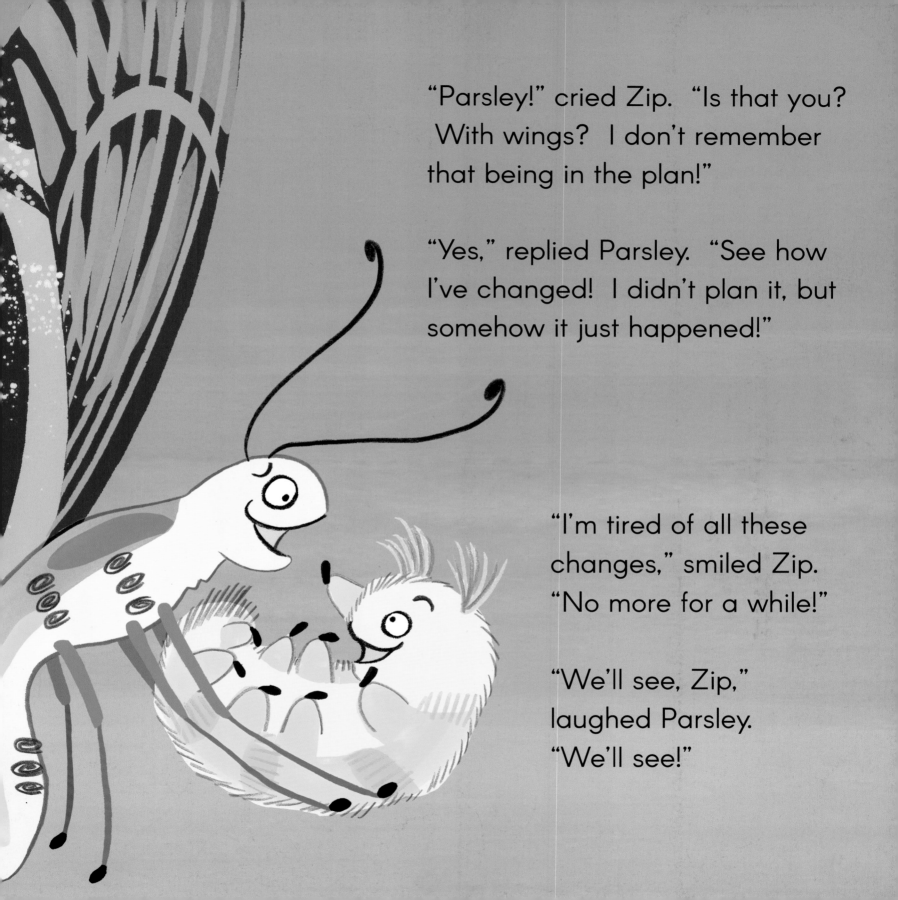

"Parsley!" cried Zip. "Is that you? With wings? I don't remember that being in the plan!"

"Yes," replied Parsley. "See how I've changed! I didn't plan it, but somehow it just happened!"

"I'm tired of all these changes," smiled Zip. "No more for a while!"

"We'll see, Zip," laughed Parsley. "We'll see!"

For Carys – K.C.

Something Else

Kathryn Cave
Illustrated by Chris Riddell

PUFFIN BOOKS

On a windy hill
alone
with nothing to be friends with
lived Something Else.

He knew that was what he was because everyone said so.

If he tried to sit with them
   or walk with them
      or join in their games,
         they always said:

"Sorry. You're not like us.
You're something else.
You don't belong."

Something Else did his best
to be like the others.

He smiled and said "Hi!" like they did.

He painted pictures.

He played their games when they let him.

He brought his lunch in a paper bag like theirs.

It was no good.

He didn't look like them
or talk like them.

He didn't see the things they saw.

He didn't play the way they played.

As for his
packed lunches...

"You don't belong here," they said.
"You're not like us. You're something else."

Something Else went home.
While he was getting ready for bed,
there was a knock on the door.

Something was standing on the doorstep.
"Hi there!" it said. "Great to meet you. Can I come in?"
"Excuse me?" said Something Else.

"You're welcome," said the creature.
It stuck out a paw, or maybe a flipper.

Something Else looked at the paw.
"I think you've come to the wrong place," he said.

The creature shook its head. "No, I haven't.
This place is perfect. Look!"

And before Something Else realized what was happening,
it walked right in...

...and sat down on his supper.

"Do I know you?" asked Something Else, puzzled.
"Know me?" The creature laughed. "Of course you do!
Take a good look. Go on!"

Something Else looked.

He walked round the creature from front to back or back to front. He didn't know what to say, so he didn't say anything.

"Don't you see?" the creature cried. "I'm just like you! You're something else, and I'M ONE TOO!" It stuck out its paw again and smiled.

Something Else was too surprised to smile back.
He didn't take the paw either.

"Like me?" he said. "You're not like me.
In fact, you're not like anything I've ever seen.
I'm sorry, but you're definitely not MY sort of something else."
He walked to the door and opened it. "Goodnight."

The creature put down its paw, slowly.
"Oh," it said.
It looked sadder and smaller.

It reminded Something Else of something,
but he couldn't think what.

While he was trying to remember, the creature left.

Then Something Else remembered.
"Wait!" he cried. "Don't go!"

He ran after the creature as fast as he could.
When he caught up, he grabbed its paw and held on tight.
"You're not like me, BUT I DON'T MIND.
You can stay with me if you'd like to."
And the creature did.

From then on, Something Else had Something to be friends with.

They smiled and said "Hi!"
to each other.

They painted pictures.

They played each other's games, or tried to.

They ate their lunches side by side.

They were different,
but they got along.

And when something turned up that really WAS weird-looking, they didn't say he wasn't like them and he didn't belong there.

They moved right up
and made room for him too.

Also in Puffin

IT WAS A DARK AND STORMY NIGHT *Janet and Allan Ahlberg*
PRINCE CINDERS *Babette Cole*
KNOCK, KNOCK, WHO'S THERE? *Sally Grindley and Anthony Browne*
PLATYPUS *Chris Riddell*
THE TRUE STORY OF THE 3 LITTLE PIGS *Jon Scieszka and Lane Smith*
THE WITCH IN THE CHERRY TREE *Margaret Mahy and Jenny Williams*

Winner of the UNESCO Prize and shortlisted for the Smarties Prize and the Kate Greenaway Medal

PUFFIN BOOKS

Published by the Penguin Group
Penguin Books Ltd, 80 Strand, London WC2R 0RL, England
Penguin Group (USA), Inc., 375 Hudson Street, New York, New York 10014, USA
Penguin Books Australia Ltd, 250 Camberwell Road, Camberwell, Victoria 3124, Australia
Penguin Books Canada Ltd, 10 Alcorn Avenue, Toronto, Ontario, Canada M4V 3B2
Penguin Books India (P) Ltd, 11 Community Centre, Panchsheel Park, New Delhi – 110 017, India
Penguin Group (NZ), cnr Airborne and Rosedale Roads, Albany, Auckland 1310, New Zealand
Penguin Books (South Africa) (Pty) Ltd, 24 Sturdee Avenue, Rosebank 2196, South Africa

Penguin Books Ltd, Registered Offices: 80 Strand, London WC2R 0RL, England

www.penguin.com

First published by Viking 1994
Published in Picture Puffins 1995
26

Text copyright © Kathryn Cave, 1994
Illustrations copyright © Chris Riddell, 1994
All rights reserved

The moral right of the author and illustrator has been asserted

Filmset in Bembo
Made and printed in Italy by Printer Trento Srl

British Library Cataloguing in Publication Data
A CIP catalogue record for this book is available from the British Library

ISBN-13: 978-0-14054-907-2